THE
SORCERER'S
APPRENTICE

THE
SORCERER'S
APPRENTICE

A Greek Fable

by

MARIANNA MAYER

with illustrations by
DAVID WIESNER

A BANTAM SKYLARK BOOK®
NEW YORK • TORONTO • LONDON • SYDNEY • AUCKLAND

THE SORCERER'S APPRENTICE
A Bantam Skylark Book / November 1989
Skylark Books is a registered trademark of Bantam Books,
a division of Bantam Doubleday Dell Publishing Group, Inc.
Registered in U.S. Patent and Trademark Office and elsewhere.

Library of Congress Catalog Card Number: 89-37432

ISBN 0-553-05844-4

Published simultaneously in the United States and Canada

Bantam Books are published by Bantam Books, a division of
Bantam Doubleday Dell Publishing Group, Inc. Its trademark,
consisting of the words "Bantam Books" and the portrayal
of a rooster, is Registered in U.S. Patent and Trademark
Office and in other countries. Marca Registrada. Bantam Books,
666 Fifth Avenue, New York, New York 10103.

PRINTED IN THE UNITED STATES OF AMERICA

WAK   0 9 8 7 6 5 4 3 2 1

For Sebastian Tillinger
M.M.

For Dilys
D.W.

Preface

HE *Sorcerer's Apprentice* is a time-less tale of the penalties and con-sequences of power in inexperienced hands. The story can be traced through eighteen hundred years and has spawned works of classical music, poetry, dramatic plays, and prose. In the second century, the brilliant Greek writer and satirist, Lucian of Samosata, included one of the earliest versions of the fable, in dialogue form, in his collection of works entitled *The Lie Fancier*. Here the sorcerer is an enigmatic character, and the impetuous apprentice is a young man and by no means a match for a company of bewitched brooms.

In subsequent versions written during the Middle Ages and the romantic era, the sorcerer was depicted as a sinister force whose powers

were derived from the black arts. Perhaps a major reason for this interpretation can be attributed to the real-life figure Dr. Johann Faustus, who lived in Germany during the sixteenth century. A magician and astrologer, Faustus was credited with supernatural powers acquired through black magic. So famous was he that after his death Johann Spies in 1587 published a nonfiction account of his life, *The History of Dr. Faustus, the Notorious Magician and Master of the Black Art.* Immediately popular, the German edition was soon translated into many other languages. No doubt the English edition was the impetus for the Elizabethan dramatist Christopher Marlowe's play *The Tragical History of Dr. Faustus*, written in 1592. Moreover, literary scholars agree that Marlowe's play was the inspiration for Goethe's verse epic, *Faust*, begun in 1772 but not completed until 1831.

Today the tale is known to a wide public through the delightful symphonic poem *L'apprenti sorcier* composed by Paul Dukas (1865–1935). The Brothers Grimm added the folktale to their collection of stories, and Walt Disney Studios turned music and story into an animated film with Mickey Mouse as the confounded apprentice.

The present version must give thanks to these sources and others, namely Edmund Spenser's

The Faerie Queen and other tales concerning Merlin, unquestionably the greatest sorcerer of them all. It was with this mythic figure in mind that I chose to name Alex's master Bleise, whose namesake residing in the county of Northumberland was believed to be Merlin's first master. In addition, the two feuding sorcerers, Bungay and Vandermast, were the names of two friends of the Franciscan monk and alchemist Roger Bacon, who was accused in the thirteenth century of practicing black magic.

It was this author's task to create a fresh tale, motivated by these sources but not rigidly based on material of the past. Instead, this story is an original tale, using old tradition as its touchstone. For this reason, *The Sorcerer's Apprentice* should be read not as a work of scholarship or adaptation, but as a work of pure imagination.

MARIANNA MAYER

Chapter One

ARLY one morning, even before the sun came up, a young boy packed his small traveling bag and set out down the dusty road. The boy's name was Alex, he was an orphan, and he made his living working at whatever honest labor came his way.

That year, from spring through autumn, Alex had worked for a farmer. Now, with the planting and harvesting season over, the farmer had no further work for the boy. So Alex was moving on to look for new employment.

By the time the sun was overhead, Alex had walked many miles and he was growing tired and

hungry. He decided to stop and rest. As he looked about for a shady place, he spied a small, weathered sign tacked up on a tree not far from where he stood.

It read,

Apprentice Wanted.
Experience not necessary. Apply in person.
Follow the brook to the stone tower.
Small salary, food, and lodging provided.
Signed, Bleise the Sorcerer.

"That's for me!" exclaimed Alex, delighted. "I do hope the position hasn't been filled already. From the look of this worn sign, I think it must've been posted a long time ago."

Indeed, the sorcerer had posted the sign a very long time ago. So long ago that he had quite forgotten that it was there any longer. But as it happened no one had applied for the position and the magician was still in need of an apprentice, even if he had forgotten all about it.

Bleise was a powerful magician, perhaps one of the most powerful. With his magic he could fetch what he pleased and perform whatever dangerous deeds he willed. He could make the simplest objects do his bidding. A wave of his hand and a few choice magic words would send a trunk to far-off India for gold, shovels to ransack the deepest oceans for lustrous pearls, and baskets to search the whole wide world for the plumpest fruit and the rarest delicacies—all this to be brought right back to the sorcerer's own tower.

The only thing the sorcerer did not use his magic for was the tending of his herb garden. This he staunchly believed must be worked by human hands alone and not by magic, for Bleise said that it was not wise to use magic in Great Art, and every sorcerer knew that herb garden-

ing was one of the greatest arts in his profession.

"Imagine," he was known to say, "the folly in making a beautiful painting by magic. Well, growing herbs for a sorcerer's magic potions, such as those used for healing, antidotes to poisons, cures of all kinds too numerous to mention, is just as vital as creating a glorious painting and must, I say, absolutely *must* be done by hand to be done properly."

So Bleise needed an apprentice to tend to his precious herb garden or he must tend to it himself. No sorcerer could do without the power of plants and still call himself a sorcerer. Now, Bleise could borrow what he needed, but that meant forever going off in one distant direction or another to borrow a sprig of this or a root of that from some other better stocked magician. And that would be humiliating, to say the least. No, Bleise needed an apprentice and he had every intention of setting out to find one—only somehow along the way he had forgotten all about it. No doubt it would come to him again. In the meantime, he tended to the garden himself with a good deal of complaining and irritation witnessed and endured by his long-suffering companion, the tawny-colored owl, Hector.

Meanwhile, as the sign had instructed, the young boy followed the brook, which led him off

the road and directly into the deep woods. By now the sun was going down and there was only a slight sound of clanking, which grew louder and louder as he walked on.

The path took Alex toward a clearing in the forest where he soon saw flickering candlelight coming from the windows of a stone tower. In the fading glow of sunset the tower was a pale column with a winding staircase that ran along the exterior walls like a slender snake and finally ringed the upper story and made a balcony.

In front of the tower there was a well where water was drawn out. The clanking noise Alex had heard was caused by a very old man who was drawing water out of the well by means of a metal bucket attached to a chain pulled up by a rather rusty, noisy crank. *Clank, bang, creak, clank,* went the crank, the chain, and the tired old bucket till at last it reached the rim of the well. All the while the old gentleman muttered to himself as he drew up the bucket. "It is a sorry state of affairs when a man of my stature and advanced age must be subjected to such indignity," said he with a furious glance at the object that was causing him such difficulty.

Alex was so astonished that he stood stock-still. The man was dressed in a flowing dark blue robe with fur trimming the edges of his very

wide sleeves. Here and there signs of the zodiac were embroidered over the fabric, with strange symbols, triangles with eyes in their centers, crosses and circles, oak leaves, and various constellations with stars and planets that shone like bits of the shining sun. On his head he wore a pointed hat not unlike a dunce's cap, only it wasn't. Tucked under one arm was a wand made from a once mighty ash tree, and upon his long, rather pointed, but not unattractive nose, he wore a pair of gold-rimmed spectacles.

"Excuse me, sir," said Alex. "I'm here about the advertisement. Can you tell me if I've come to the right place?"

The aged gentleman looked up from what he was doing and gazed at the boy for a long moment without answering.

At last he said, "Your name would be . . . Alex."

"Yes, sir," said the boy, more surprised than ever. "Pleased to meet you, sir."

"My name," said the old sorcerer, "is Bleise. Perhaps you've heard of me and perhaps you haven't."

"Why, no. That is to say, how do you do, sir. Pleased to have the honor, sir, I'm sure."

"Likewise, lad."

Even after speaking, the magician continued

17

to stare at the boy with an unblinking and kindly interest which made Alex feel that it was quite all right to do the same.

Bleise had a flowing white beard and a long white moustache which hung down lankly on either side of his mouth. His large blue eyes behind the gold-rimmed spectacles were surely the most astonishing feature in an altogether remarkable looking gentleman, for they were piercing blue like the brightest, bluest sky. Indeed, as the two gazed at each other, it seemed to Alex that the sorcerer could look right into him and through him, that he could see into the far future and the distant past as clearly as he saw this little boy standing rather uncertainly before him.

All at once Bleise shook his head as though he had tried to remember something he had forgotten.

"Never mind, it will come to me, I'm sure. All in due time," said the magician with a shrug of his shoulders. Then he added, "Are you hungry?" and with that he abruptly walked off in the direction of the tower, still straining with the weight of the water bucket.

"Very, sir. Yes, I am," answered Alex as he followed after, since this seemed the only thing to do. He offered to carry the bucket, which

pleased the sorcerer, who gave it to him with a smile.

Relieved of his burden, the sorcerer removed his tall pointed hat and began to mop his brow with a rather dingy pocket handkerchief. As he did, he tipped his hat and a mouse fell out that looked as though it had been dead for quite some time. Just then a tawny-colored owl swooped down to snatch the tasty morsel, but the sorcerer said, "Hector, stop that at once. You must wait till supper. You've had far too many snacks already."

The owl made a quick turn in mid-flight and with an apologetic screech flew up into one of the open tower windows. The boy was so startled to see such antics that he stopped in his tracks and stared openmouthed. The sorcerer turned back to look at Alex with a sly smile. "I wonder, would you be in the market for a bit of work?"

Chapter Two

NCE INSIDE, Alex could see that the tower was divided into three separate sections. The lower level, where he and the sorcerer had entered, had a kitchen, storeroom, and dining room. On the second story there were two large bedrooms, each with its own study. And finally there was the uppermost room, where Bleise labored to perform high spells and mighty magic.

Still carrying the water bucket Alex climbed up the staircase after his host to the uppermost room. There he found himself in the most wonderful laboratory he could have imagined. The owl, Hector, was hanging upside down from his

perch, and when his master entered, he winked one amber eye in greeting. Obviously, thought Alex, he held no grudge even if he had been deprived of a treat.

Everywhere Alex looked there were books. Thousands of brown and vermilion leather-bound copies with gold lettering and gilt-edged pages stood on bookshelves. Others were propped against one another on the floor, and still more were piled high, one on top of the other, in shaky stacks that threatened to tumble at the slightest touch but somehow didn't.

There were small flame burners, crystal balls, silkworms spinning silk, ancient skulls, prisms, and cauldrons of every size. Green, ruby, purple, and silver liquids bubbled in glass phials and beakers—all of them magic potions of the highest quality.

In the center of the room a large fire blazed and gave off a warm, welcoming glow. The smoke from the flames came curling up through a hole in the tower roof made expressly for that purpose. Over on the windowsill tiny herb seedlings were growing. Above the plants was a huge circular window that looked out on the forest far below and the dark blue star-studded sky with its luminous full moon so close that Alex thought he could reach out and touch it.

23

"Here, lad. Bring that water bucket over to the seedlings. They need watering. These plants and those growing in my garden are for my various preparations. I would use magic to tend them if it were possible, instead of struggling with this confounded labor. But I'm afraid that magic would upset their vital properties. You see, lad, the balance of nature does not take kindly to too much magic without becoming upset."

Alex nodded his head in agreement, even though he was not at all sure he did understand. But the boy watered the seedlings carefully and smiled up at the sorcerer, whom he already liked very much indeed, even if he didn't quite follow everything he said.

"It will be your job to take care of my plants and to weed, water, and generally look after the herb garden. Do you think you can manage that?" asked the sorcerer.

"Yes, sir. Certainly. I know a good deal about gardening."

"Very good, then. It is settled. I'm so glad I found you, or rather that you found me. I'll show you your room and then to dinner."

That evening, dinner was neatly laid out for two in the dining room. There was a savory stew with parsley dumplings and all kinds of other

good things to eat. For dessert there was cherry pie with ice cream and the very best chocolate cake Alex ever tasted.

"Will you have some salt and pepper with your stew?" asked Master Bleise. But before Alex could reach for them, both shakers came trotting over to his end of the table and sprinkled themselves over his meal.

"They *are* marvelous!" gasped Alex in amazement.

The pair were so delighted at the boy's words of praise that they tipped themselves over for an

elaborate bow that left salt and pepper all over the tablecloth.

Master Bleise sneezed, and then softly rapped the table with his knuckles. The salt and pepper shakers immediately snapped to attention. "Yes, they're a fine pair, but a bit too fond of compliments, I see."

After dinner, Alex got up to clear the table, but the sorcerer told him not to bother. Instead, with a wave of his hand and a word Alex didn't quite catch, the cups and saucers, plates, forks and knives, leftovers, and everything else picked themselves up and scurried off toward the sink in the kitchen. From that room, Alex heard shouting and clamoring as though a crowd of children had suddenly gathered to have a dip in their favorite swimming hole.

Chapter Three

HE FOLLOWING weeks went splendidly and the new apprentice tended to the herb garden with eagerness. He worked hard hauling water from the well, and he hoed and weeded, but it was not too difficult, since the sorcerer's magic took care of all the other chores. The laundry, housecleaning, cooking, and washing up were all done by magical powers, although the sorcerer's apprentice never saw any magic actually summoned.

Then, late one summer night, after the young apprentice had worked for his master many months, he was awakened by the sound of thunder. The noise was so fierce that Alex could only think that a terrible storm was brewing.

Suddenly he remembered with a start that the window in his master's workroom was open. Up he jumped from his bed, for he had to shut the window at once or the new crop of seedlings on the windowsill would surely be damaged by the stormy winds.

Climbing the stairs three steps at a time, Alex quickly reached the room and burst in. But there was the sorcerer, standing in the center of a drawn circle on the floor. His eyes were shut, his arms were held high, and with his magic wand whirling wildly in the air, he was fighting or summoning (Alex couldn't tell which) lightning and thunder, whirlwind and tempest. It was an awesome sight, to say the least.

Stunned, Alex quickly took cover under the table. What could it all mean? Truly Alex didn't know what to think or do. But as the crack of lightning and the roar of thunder grew more terrible, he began to fear for his master. At last, throwing caution aside, he sprang out of his hiding place. Without a thought for his own safety, he ran forward and grasped hold of his master's sleeve.

Suddenly there was a most extraordinary explosion. A thick cloud of blue smoke came billowing up from out of nowhere to encircle the pair. The walls grew hazy and melted away.

The tower roof opened wide with a mighty crack and disappeared altogether.

At that moment, Alex felt himself rising straight up and out of what remained of the sorcerer's workroom. He waved his arms and legs; there was nothing to stop his flight. In seconds he felt a cool rush of night air against his face. The smoke changed to a heavy mist that clung to him, and try as he might, he was quite unable to see beyond it.

"I'm flying!" he exclaimed to no one in particular. But where was he bound for? He had no idea.

He still had hold of the end of his master's sleeve. He gave it a tug and called out, hoping for an answer. There was no reply.

He didn't have time to worry about this, for just then his flight took on quite a different direction. To his dismay, Alex began to fall. Down, down, down he went. Gently, slowly, but decidedly down. His descent went on for so long that he began to think it would never end.

Tiny silver specks appeared in the mist and began swirling around his head like a thousand swarming insects. Alex grew dizzy with their incessant buzzing. And so it was with very great relief that suddenly he felt his feet touch down on something solid, and in the next second he

found himself sitting upon a nice soft mound of grass.

Happily, he had arrived safe and sound. The mist began to lift and soon vanished without a trace. Alex's first thought was for the sorcerer, but he was quite alone. As to what remained of Master Bleise's sleeve, all that Alex held in his grasp was a tattered fragment of cloth torn away from the esteemed gentleman's cuff.

"Well, he can't be far off," thought Alex. "I shall just have to have a look."

It was only then that Alex gave serious consideration to his new surroundings. Indeed, what he saw was new to him, for he was in a forest unlike any he had ever seen before.

"How beautiful it is!" exclaimed Alex. And so it was. Every color and shape was alive and glowing with a magic light that shimmered. The forest murmured in his ears and the breath of spring was everywhere. He ran his hand down the bark of one tree. It was made of pure gold, and diamonds were scattered upon the leaves like morning dew. The pebbles and stones and boulders were of luminous alabaster, and a silver stream flowed close by. Crimson flowers on long, slender turquoise stems grew along the mossy banks of the stream, and Alex, fascinated, leaned down to study them more closely. Just then the

blossoms lifted their delicate heads and fixed a steady gaze on him.

At that same moment, Alex heard his master's voice, saying, "Now, I know it must be somewhere near here."

Following the sound, Alex was just able to catch a glimpse of the sorcerer as he stepped through an opening carved out of the side of a vine-covered mountain. Alex hurried after him and soon found himself in a darkened tunnel. It was a gloomy place and Alex hesitated to call out, not knowing what else he might disturb. Up ahead he saw a glimmer of light, and Alex headed for it. After a few steps along the twisting passage, Alex spied his master once more. But he was doing something curious, and again caution made Alex hang back and wait.

He saw at once that the light he had followed emanated from a wood-burning fire under a large cauldron. The sorcerer lifted an iron spoon from out of the cauldron. Three drops fell from the edge of the spoon. He caught them up with his finger and put his finger to his lips. As he tasted it, an odd expression came over his face and a light came into his brilliant blue eyes.

Suddenly there was a terrible shout, and out sprang a witch the size of a giant. She shrieked when she saw the sorcerer and lunged for him.

"You've stolen the three precious drops of wisdom," growled the giantess. "Mark my words, Bleise. You shan't get away from me now!"

But the sorcerer turned in the nick of time and fled down the tunnel. Once outside he turned himself into a hare. The giantess was not fooled. She in turn changed herself into a sleek greyhound and chased after him. Just as she was about to snatch the hare in her jaws, the hare changed into a fish and jumped into the stream. The hound turned into an otter and dove into the water. When the otter was about to seize hold of the fish, the fish changed into a bird, and up it soared out of the water and flew into the air. Quickly the otter turned into a hawk and flew in swift pursuit. But the bird changed into a tiny grain of wheat and let itself fall down into a pile of grain that lay in a field. The witch took her own shape once more and gathered the grain. All this Alex watched at a safe distance; in the excitement he had not been noticed.

Grumbling to herself, the witch gathered every single kernel of grain and took it home. She ground it and turned it into flour. She mixed it into dough and kneaded it into a loaf. She left it to rise and then she kneaded it again. At last, she placed the loaf in a pan and put it into a hot oven.

Soon enough it was baked, and when she removed it from the oven it was a beautiful golden loaf of bread. This the witch placed on the windowsill to cool, saying, "I'll get those three drops yet, Bleise. I'll eat this whole loaf when it cools and will have devoured you and the three drops of wisdom in the bargain."

Alex had seen and heard it all. When the witch was out of sight, he crept to the window and stole the bread.

"Oh, Master Bleise, I hope you are in there," he said to the bread.

"I daresay *I am*!" said a familiar voice from inside the loaf. "Break open the bread, like a good lad, and see for yourself."

Open it he did and out came the sorcerer. At first he was only a tiny speck of a person, but then he grew and grew, larger and larger, until he was quite himself again.

"Now, then, Alex, my splendid lad!" said the sorcerer as he straightened his hat and dusted flour from the folds of his robe. Alex could see he was rather out of breath and red-cheeked with excitement after his long ordeal. "We must be on our way and at once. I'll wager that I'll be a fire-breathing dragon if that old witch won't be after us in a snap, once she discovers I've escaped."

"A fire-breathing dragon, indeed!" exclaimed Alex with a laugh. "Master, I'll wager that with your powerful magic, you could be anything at all!"

With a laugh in return, the sorcerer took hold of Alex's hand, and in an instant they were up in the air and gone from sight. In no time flat, they were back in the tower. The walls, the roof, the workroom, everything was exactly as it had been before the explosion.

That day the sorcerer was filled with praise for Alex, and he thanked the boy most sincerely for handling his rescue so cleverly.

"I can't think that you wouldn't have come up with something to get away," said Alex, modestly.

"I suppose I would have before too long," replied the sorcerer, with a twinkle in his eye. "But all the same, my good lad, it's certainly nice to have a friend when you're in need."

"All those changes," Alex inquired, shyly. "They were *all magic*, weren't they, sir?"

"Why, yes, my boy. Indeed, they were all magic, of course," answered the sorcerer with a broad smile.

Left to himself, Alex thought his adventure had been marvelous. In fact, the sorcerer's apprentice couldn't remember when he had had a better time. He decided that it would certainly

be worth his while to observe his talented master very carefully in future. Perhaps his master was not altogether prepared to share his magic, but Alex couldn't help believing that such remarkable powers would be a handy thing for a boy to learn.

"Certainly," he thought, "a boy never knows when the art of magic might be quite useful to him."

From that day forward Alex trained a watchful eye on his master, and whenever he was sure to be alone, he drew down from the bookshelves the great volumes used for weaving spells. Unfortunately these books taught him very little, since most were in languages he didn't understand. But this was soon to change quite abruptly.

One afternoon while Alex was working out-of-doors, he was startled by the sound of clanging coming from the well. When he looked around, he saw a quite ordinary broom carrying away a bucket filled with water. Alex followed the broom as it turned and marched toward the tower. There it climbed up the outside staircase to the sorcerer's workroom, whereupon it opened the balcony door, walked into the room, and shut the door behind it with a bang.

The next afternoon the very same scene was repeated. So on the third afternoon Alex, burn-

ing with curiosity, was determined to find out how his master could make a broom do his bidding. Without his master noticing, he crept into the hallway and overheard the magic words that brought the broom to life.

"BAGABI AQUA LACA BACHABE!" chanted the sorcerer and then he clapped his hands three times. Suddenly, the broom stood up and two thin arms sprouted. As if this was not enough, out of nowhere a bucket materialized. The broom

picked up the bucket and then straight as a soldier spun around and marched off to the well. When the coast was clear Alex hurried to his own room, where he wrote down the spell so he would not forget it.

Chapter Four

FEW evenings later, a messenger arrived with a note for Bleise. After reading it, the sorcerer told Alex, "My two oldest friends, Bungay and Vandermast, are having another one of their feuds and I must go mediate or something terrible might happen.

"The last time, their disagreement resulted in Bungay casting a spell that sent poor Vandermast into the lake just as he was having tea and toast with his elderly aunt. When he swam out of the water, Vandermast was so enraged that he raised several evil-looking spirits to carry Bungay off. But, at last, I managed to calm them both so that no real harm was done, and much to my relief they did agree to be friends again,"

Bleise sighed deeply and went on to say, "Now I fear they are arguing once more. So I must go and see what can be done to restore peace." Then the sorcerer's expression brightened as he said, "Never mind, Alex, I shan't be away long. In fact, I should be back the morning after next, if everything goes well. But while I'm gone, I'm afraid you'll be left to look after everything. You see, there'll be no magic to do the chores while I'm away. I hope you don't mind too much?"

"Don't worry, Master Bleise. When you return you'll find everything right as rain," said Alex with confidence. "Just leave it to me, you won't be sorry you did."

Bright and early next morning, Bleise summoned his transportation for the journey. In a cloud of thick green smoke a griffin flew down and said, "Climb aboard." As soon as the smoke cleared, the sorcerer did just that and made himself comfortable. Then, with many fond farewells to his apprentice, the sorcerer flew into the sky on the back of his griffin. Alex waved goodbye till they were out of sight and then he set to work.

It was very warm that morning and Alex hurried to get all his gardening done before midday, when it would be far too hot to work outside. He carried water from the well. It was hard work, for the plants were very thirsty in the heat and he had to make many trips. When at last the watering and weeding were finished, it was nearly noon.

Alex went inside for lunch and found the dirty breakfast dishes waiting to be washed and the house quite a mess. His master had left in such a great rush that everything was upside down.

"No matter," said Alex with a shrug of his shoulders. "Even without my master's magic to help, I'll see to the mess; it'll just take time. But first I must have something to eat."

After lunch he began washing the breakfast and lunch dishes. But no sooner was he ready to rinse than he saw that the water barrel was completely empty and needed to be filled.

"Oh, no!" groaned Alex. He had managed to cover himself and the dishes in soap and there was not a drop of clean water to rinse with. "I must go straight out and draw fresh water from the well or there shall be no water at all. Unless . . ."—all at once an idea occurred to him—"I get the broom to fetch the water."

Alex wondered if he dare try. Would the sorcerer be furious if he found out? "Why should he be?" wondered the apprentice as he eyed the broom that leaned against the kitchen wall. "Surely my master would have done it himself if he hadn't been in such a hurry this morning. And anyway, Master Bleise need never know anything about it."

Without giving himself another moment to change his mind, Alex said, *"BAGABI AQUA LACA BACHABE!"* Then he clapped his hands three times, just as he remembered his master had done.

At first the broom was perfectly still. But presently it jerked itself straight up to stand before Alex. The apprentice jumped back and gasped, "Oh, it's working! I've actually done it!"

A thin wooden arm appeared on either side of the broom. A bucket materialized out of the air. The broom stretched out its two arms and picked up the bucket. Then it turned and rushed up the stairs and out the door. Off it went to the well to fetch water. The sorcerer's apprentice had worked his first magic spell, seemingly without difficulty.

Alex was still marveling at his newfound power when the broom returned. Just for a moment it stood at the top of the stairs with a full bucket of water. Alex pointed to the water bar-

rel to be filled. But the broom flung the water across the room, drenching Alex and everything else. Then it was off before Alex could stop it.

"Oh, this won't do at all," said Alex. "Next time I shall speak to the broom."

In a flash, the broom was back with fresh water. Alex said, "Empty the bucket into the barrel, like a good fellow." Before all the words were out of his mouth, the broom threw the water not into the barrel but into the room, and was off again to fetch more.

"All right then, I must make sure to get the

bucket away from the broom before any more water is spilt." As soon as the broom came back, Alex made a leap for the bucket. But the broom was too quick for him and the water was thrown over his head.

"Something is terribly wrong here," said Alex as he wiped water off his face with the end of his very damp shirt sleeve. "I had better haul the water myself or there will surely be a flood."

So when the broom returned, Alex said with authority, *"BAGABI AQUA LACA BACHABE! Stop bringing water!"* and clapped his hands three times. The broom paid him no attention whatever and flung the water into the room. Again it rushed away for more.

Alex became desperate—he had to find a way to stop the broom. He saw an axe beside the woodpile. He took it up and swung at the broom, splitting it in two. But instead of stopping it, the two halves suddenly turned into *two* brooms, each with its own set of arms and each carrying a bucket. Off the pair went to bring back twice as much water.

The kitchen began to fill with water. Higher and higher the water level rose until it was above Alex's knees. Everything—tables, chairs, bottles, crockery, and books—began floating about the room.

Alex pleaded with the brooms to stop. He chanted the magic spell backward and forward, but it made no difference. The words were useless to stop the brooms and the water continued to rise.

"I must chop them into little pieces, then they'll have to stop," thought Alex, frantically.

With the axe, he chopped and chopped, hoping to turn the brooms into pieces as small as toothpicks. Each blow met its mark and split the brooms in half. But soon there were four, then six, eight, ten, and then twelve brooms rushing off with buckets to the well. At last, Alex stopped. It was no use; all this only made matters even worse. Now instead of one broom throwing water into the tower, there were a dozen!

Chapter Five

N NO TIME the water was so high
that Alex was forced to swim in
order to keep his head above wa-
ter. The steps that led to the second floor were
almost entirely submerged. To avoid being swal-
lowed by the flood, the brooms had now taken
to the outer staircase that wound around the
tower's exterior wall. So when they had filled
the first floor with water, the brooms climbed to
the second story and tossed water through every
open window they could reach.

Clearly the brooms were not going to stop. If
Alex didn't find a solution soon, the entire tower

would be flooded. He swam to the steps that still remained above water. Taking hold of the railing, he managed to hoist himself out of the water and onto the second floor.

Alex ran up to the sorcerer's workroom. There he was met by the sober gaze of Hector, the owl. "Hooooo," said Hector with a look of stern disapproval.

"Oh, please, Hector. Don't start hooting at me now," pleaded Alex as he hurriedly pulled book after book down from the shelves. "I must find a magic spell that will stop the brooms.

There has to be something I can use in one of these books."

Hector flapped his wings and flew off the perch. As he made his way toward the open window, the owl looked back at Alex and said, "Boys should not play with magic, if they *know-hooo* what's good for them. But all the same, good luck and goodbye," and with that he flew straight out the window.

Alex dropped the book he was holding and ran to the window, saying, "I didn't know you could talk! Oh, come back, Hector. Maybe you know what I should do to make the brooms stop." But Hector was long gone and there was no one else to help.

While Alex stood by helplessly, the brooms climbed the exterior staircase to the balcony and threw buckets of water in through the upper windows. Back and forth to the well went the twelve brooms, bringing more and more water.

"What am I going to do," wondered Alex in dismay, for he did not find a spell to stop the brooms in the first book he opened. There were spells for making rainbows, and spells for making rain. He quickly turned the pages of another book. Here was a spell for making a cow jump over the moon. Spells for removing the spots from leopards, spells for causing elephants to fly,

but not one spell for turning water-hauling brooms back into ordinary brooms. Alex picked up another book. There were spells for turning oneself into a cat, a fly, a toad, a mouse, and a medium-sized dragon of the common variety. No, no, this wasn't what he wanted.

In all this time Alex found nothing that could help, and when he looked to see how high the water level was, his heart sank. The twelve brooms, having already flooded the first and second floors, were now doing a splendid job of flooding the uppermost room.

"Tomorrow morning the sorcerer will arrive home to find the tower and all his precious belongings underwater. And he'll know at once that it's all my fault. He'll probably turn me into a worm or a slug or something even worse for my punishment. If nothing else, he'll certainly turn me out! And who could blame him. Oh, I must find the answer before he returns."

There was no doubt that Alex was frightened of the sorcerer's anger, but most of all he dreaded to have his master know that he couldn't be trusted. In the time the boy had worked for his master they had come to be quite fond of each other and Alex wished with all his heart never to lose his friendship.

Turning away from the bookshelves, Alex

searched the room for other books of magic. On the floor, he found a great, thick volume leaning against the side of the writing desk. It was chained to one of the legs, and try as he might, Alex could not budge it. So he squeezed under the desk to read the title: *THE BOOK OF EXTRAORDINARY SPELLS AND INCANTATIONS FROM A TO Z.* "This must be a dictionary," said Alex.

He quickly thumbed to the letter B for *broom*. There, at the top of the page, were spells for making a broom fly, of course! Alex read on. There were spells for turning brooms into princesses and a spell for making a *broom fetch water*! And right under it was . . . how to reverse such a spell. "At last!" shouted Alex. "I'm saved."

He read, " 'To reverse a broom under the spell of hauling water back into an ordinary broom say, *"LAMAE AQUA CACHI ACABABE"* while clapping your hands three times. Repeat as often as needed.' "

In his excitement Alex jumped up and banged his head on the bottom of the desktop. "Ouch!" he yelled. Never mind, he was in much too much of a hurry to worry about a bump on the head. He squeezed out from under the desk as quickly as he could without bumping his head for a second time and then scrambled to his feet.

For the first time all day luck was on Alex's side, for at that very moment all twelve brooms were standing on the balcony at the same time and were just about to throw their buckets of water in through the windows.

Alex rushed to the center of the room, took a deep breath, and shouted as loudly as he could, *"LAMAE AQUA CACHI ACABABE,"* as he clapped his hands three times.

All at once, the brooms began to disappear. One by one, they were gone until just a single solitary broom remained.

The broom turned away from the window with its bucket to hurry down the stairs. But Alex called after it, *"LAMAE AQUA CACHI ACABABE,"* and clapped his hands three times. The broom stopped in its tracks and stood frozen. The water bucket vanished. The broom's arms melted into thin air. For a moment the broom began to sway this way and that. Then it fell down, down, down the stairs and finally landed with a thump on the grass far below.

Alex breathed a sigh of relief. All the brooms were gone; they would not be bringing any more water. *"Water!"* he shouted. "How am I going to get rid of all this water?"

Alex rushed back to the book that had saved him from the brooms. This time he decided to look under C for *clean up*. There was a spell for cleaning a flea, a spell for cleaning the inside of a crystal ball, and finally an all-purpose spell for cleaning up an unpleasant situation, be it animal, mineral, vegetable, or anything household. Alex guessed this was the very one he should try. Just to be on the safe side, he read further to check for another incantation that could reverse it if need be. Indeed, there was one, so Alex felt it was safe to try.

He read, " 'To clean up an unpleasant situation say, *"NIX, DIX, BEGONE AND AWAY!"*

Then stamp your left foot three times while holding your right earlobe with two fingers of your left hand.' "

Alex stood up and said, *"NIX, DIX, BE-GONE AND AWAY!"* and proceeded to carry out the rest of the instructions down to the very last detail. But, at the end, just for good measure, he added a very earnest *"PLEASE."*

Just like magic, the water vanished in a flash of lightning. The tower was as dry as a bone, and a very dry bone at that. Alex could have jumped for joy, but he was too exhausted for that and there was still work to be done. Going from floor to floor, room to room, he hurried to straighten up.

By nightfall everything was put in its place and Alex was finally able to collapse in an armchair. As he dozed off, Hector flew in through the open window and perched upon Alex's shoulder. "That's a good lad. I knew you could do it, Alex," said the tawny owl as he nibbled the boy's ear affectionately.

Chapter Six

LEX DIDN'T KNOW how long he had been asleep. But the sun was already up and Hector was gently pecking at his shoulder to wake him. He opened his eyes and saw his master walk through the door, holding the broom. At the sight of the dreaded broom, Alex's face went white. He jumped out of the chair and said, "Master! I . . . ah . . . I mean . . . Welcome home!"

Bleise gave his apprentice a mysterious smile before turning away to lean the broom up against the wall. "Thank you, Alex. It's good to be home again. But, tell me, is there something wrong? You look as though you've seen a ghost."

"Oh, it's nothing like that, sir," answered Alex, nervously. "I must have fallen asleep in

this chair last night. Hector was just waking me as you came in. I guess I wasn't quite awake."

"Well, then, let's have some breakfast. I'm famished," said the sorcerer as he started toward the kitchen.

Alex followed behind his master, stopping only to look round at the broom that remained just where Bleise had left it. Hector made what sounded like an encouraging hoot at Alex and then went flying ahead to the kitchen.

"My, doesn't everything look tip-top," remarked the sorcerer as he surveyed the kitchen. "You've certainly done a good job while I've been away, my boy. I hope it wasn't too difficult for you?"

"Yes, sir. I mean no, sir. That is, there's something I must confess, Master Bleise," said Alex in a great rush.

But his master raised a hand to stop him, saying with a laugh, "Surely it can wait till we've sat down to breakfast."

Bleise waved his wand over the table and suddenly a number of covered dishes appeared out of nowhere. "Now let me see," said the sorcerer as he lifted a cover from one of the dishes. "Hmm, here are some scrambled eggs, I expect. And hot buttered toast. Smells delicious. And what do we have here? Pancakes and

maple syrup! Oh, yes, this will be a wonderful feast. Look, Alex, muffins and gooseberry jam. Your favorite!"

"Yes, sir," answered Alex with a heavy voice.

"Well then, sit down, my boy, and eat. I'm sure all that extra work while I was gone has helped to increase your appetite."

Alex sat down, looking for all the world as though he would never eat anything ever again. The sorcerer studied his apprentice. He raised his long, bony index finger and rested it along the flat of his nose the way he always did when thinking about something in particular. His bright blue eyes twinkled behind his spectacles as he leaned back in his chair. Then he removed his spectacles and began slowly to clean the lenses with the edge of his wide sleeve.

Alex looked miserable. The interruption of breakfast had made him lose his courage to confess. Now he didn't know how he should begin.

"Alex, my lad," said Master Bleise, "I've been wondering. Do you suppose you'd care for some instruction concerning magic making? I daresay, I've been thinking you might have some talent along those lines, and with training . . ."

Well, there it was, thought Alex, it's now or never. Alex shook his head sadly and said, "No,

sir. I don't think you should waste your time on me. I'm afraid I'd make an awful mess of it. In fact, sir . . . you see, I've tried some magic. I know I shouldn't have. I suppose you'll send me away now. I can't blame you. But I didn't realize my stupidity till it was too late."

Alex looked away. His cheeks burned with shame. Well, at least he had told the truth. He would be sent away and now he would never, never learn magic properly like a real apprentice. His eyes filled and a big tear started to fall.

"Oh, I don't know," said the sorcerer with a serious expression upon his face. "I think you did a rather good job with those brooms under the circumstances."

Alex shot a glance at his master. *"Brooms!* Sir, do you mean that you *know* about the brooms?"

"Now, Alex, what kind of wizard do you suppose I'd be if I didn't know what was *going* to happen and what *has* happened," exclaimed Master Bleise with a merry laugh. "It's very useful, I assure you. In time, I imagine, I'll even be able to teach you that, if you promise to be an attentive apprentice.

"Enough said. We should have our breakfast. I can't be keeping it hot all morning. And then you shall have your first *official* lesson."

"Hoooray!" hooted Hector as he flew down to join them.

Suddenly Alex realized he had a tremendous appetite. The sorcerer and his apprentice dug into their breakfast, and as they ate Master Bleise told Alex all about his adventures while he had been away.

After breakfast there was magic instruction, but both the sorcerer and Hector agreed that Alex should wait before tackling any lessons involving brooms or water for a little while anyway. Alex was only too happy to agree with his friends.

MARIANNA MAYER is one of the country's foremost storytellers of fairy tales, folktales, and myths. She is the author of over two dozen books for young readers, with over one-half million copies in print. Her books include *My First Book of Nursery Tales*, illustrated by William Joyce; *A Boy, a Dog, a Frog and a Friend* with Mercer Mayer; and *The Brambleberrys*® animal books illustrated by Caldecott winner Gerald McDermott. Her fairy tales include *Beauty and the Beast*, illustrated by Mercer Mayer; *The Unicorn and the Lake*, illustrated by Michael Hague; *The Ugly Duckling*, illustrated by Thomas Locker; and most recently *The Twelve Dancing Princesses*, illustrated by K.Y. Craft. In addition, she has written THE PRINCE AND THE PRINCESS, illustrated by Jacqueline Rogers, another book in her continuing series for Bantam Books.

DAVID WIESNER's work has been exhibited in galleries in New York City. Recent books he has illustrated include *The Loathsome Dragon*, retold with Kim Hahng; *Firebrat*, written by Nancy Willard; and *Free Fall*, which he both wrote and illustrated, and which was named a Caldecott Honor Book in 1989. Mr. Wiesner lives in Brooklyn, New York.

64